Petals, Poison and Peril

A Thorne Sister Sleuths Cozy Mystery

D.G. Thomas

Mattison Savage Publishing

ISBN: 9798306518244

ACKNOWLEDGMENTS

CONTENTS

Prologue

The Sisters of Blossom & Thorne

The gentle hum of the floral cooler filled the quiet of *Blossom & Thorne*, the rhythm as familiar to me as my own heartbeat. Sunlight streamed through the shop's wide display windows, casting a golden glow across the neat rows of vases brimming with fresh-cut blooms. The air, rich with the scent of roses and eucalyptus, carried a warmth that had nothing to do with the temperature.

For me and my sister, Poppy, this

shop wasn't just a business. It was home.

Quite literally.

Our lives had been rooted in *Blossom & Thorne* since childhood. We grew up in the apartments above the shop, the walls infused with the ever-present perfume of lilies and lavender. Even now, as adults, we still lived there—our lives woven together by shared memories and the day-to-day demands of running the business.

In one apartment, I lived with my twelve-year-old son, Phillip, my refuge built on structure, quiet moments, and the careful order I carved into each day. Next door, my younger sister Poppy lived in happy chaos with her husband, Scott, and their spirited five-year-old daughter, Violet, their home filled with giggles, the pitter-patter of tiny feet, and the occasional explosion of glitter.

Our mother had built this shop from the ground up. She poured her heart into every bouquet, teaching us not just how to arrange flowers, but how to listen to what people needed — to craft something meaningful with our hands. When she passed, keeping the shop alive wasn't just an obligation. It was a promise. A way to hold onto the pieces of her we weren't ready to let go.

Even now, as I stood behind the counter, trimming the stems of fresh roses with precise, practiced hands, I could almost hear her voice. *Make sure every flower has room to breathe, sweetheart. Let them shine.*

I was meticulous, a perfectionist to the core. Customers often joked that my bouquets told stories, each arrangement a carefully curated balance of color and texture. Poppy, ever the dreamer, had a different approach. She leaned into bold, unconventional designs, playing with contrast and movement in a way that could win over even the most difficult clients. If I was the roots that kept us grounded, Poppy was the petals that added flourish.

It worked.

Most of the time.

Life in a small town, however, wasn't always as picturesque as our shop's cozy, flower-filled interior. Bloomwood had its charm, but it was also the kind of place where privacy was a luxury. Everyone knew everyone's business, and news—whether true or twisted—spread like wildflowers in spring.

Over the years, Poppy and I had learned how to navigate it, carefully choosing what parts of our lives we let others see.

But sometimes, no matter how well you prepare, things spiral beyond your control.

Looking back, the signs had been there. Subtle, like the way a rose wilts just before its petals fall. What started as an ordinary week — unpacking a new shipment of flowers, preparing arrangements for an upcoming gala, tending to the usual bustle of customers — would unravel into something far more sinister.

Secrets. Betrayal. Murder.

For now, though, I focused on my work, oblivious to the storm gathering just beyond our doors. My only concern at that moment was whether our next shipment of orchids would arrive on time.

I was wrong.

Because even in a flower shop as warm and welcoming as *Blossom & Thorne*, not everything was as innocent as it seemed.

Chapter 1

Blooming Trouble

The scent of fresh-brewed coffee mingled with the subtle perfume of flowers drifting up from the shop below. The morning hum of life in the apartments above *Blossom & Thorne* had already begun—water running through the pipes, soft footsteps padding across wooden floors, and Poppy's voice carrying through the narrow stairwell.

"Iris, do you have any of Phillip's socks over there? I swear, they keep vanishing!"

I sighed, adjusting the strap of my robe before reaching for my own lukewarm coffee. "I barely have matching socks for myself, Poppy."

Across the kitchen, Phillip slumped over a bowl of cereal, lazily shoveling spoonfuls into his mouth with the enthusiasm of a kid who'd rather still be asleep. His curly hair was sticking up in all directions, and his uniform shirt — despite my best efforts — was slightly wrinkled. I considered making him change but let it go. I was picking my battles this morning.

Scott's voice floated from Poppy's apartment as he wrangled Violet into her sneakers. "Alright, munchkin, let's move. If we leave now, we'll have time for the 'Super Secret Spy Mission' on the way to school."

Violet squealed in delight. "Do I get to use my invisible shield?"

"Of course. But only if we hurry."

I glanced at Phillip, who rolled his eyes as he shoved another spoonful of cereal into his mouth. "Lucky Violet. I never got spy missions on my way to school."

I smirked and reached for his backpack, handing it to him. "Your dad used to do them when you were little."

He shrugged. "Yeah, but it's cooler when you can actually remember them."

I pressed a kiss to the top of his head before nudging him toward the door. "Bus won't wait, kid. Let's go."

Once Phillip was out the door, I took a deep breath and let the morning settle. These moments—before the shop opened, before the customers came with their orders, their expectations — were my favorite. Mornings held a kind of clarity, a reset button before the weight of the day set in.

But today, something felt... off. Pushing away the thought, I grabbed my bag and invoices and headed downstairs.

Poppy was already in her usual spot at the ancient desktop computer, clicking with the kind of determination usually reserved for coaxing stubborn old dogs or printers from 1998. The screen flickered once, as if reconsidering its life choices, and then resumed its slow crawl through the day's invoices.

The shop smelled like lilies and fresh eucalyptus, the scent wrapping around me like a well-worn blanket—comforting and familiar, despite the low buzz of tension that had followed us all week.

"Morning," I said, setting my bag behind the counter.

Poppy didn't look up. "Morning. You just missed the Reverend—he stopped in a few minutes ago to pick up that sympathy arrangement for the Maxwell funeral."

"Already?" I blinked. "That man is quicker than the delivery van."

"Also," she added, glancing at a Post-it stuck to the edge of the monitor, "Mayor Whitfield's assistant came in yesterday afternoon. Wanted an update on the centerpieces for the gala. Apparently, they're 'crucial to the entire aesthetic experience.'"

I raised an eyebrow. "Did he say it like that?"

Poppy smirked. "Exactly like that. With jazz hands."

I laughed, rolled my eyes and moved toward the front window to straighten a leaning display of potted herbs. The bell above the door jingled behind me.

"Morning, Maggie," Poppy called out cheerfully.

Maggie Bishop—owner of Maggie's Café and queen of brisk sass—strode into the shop wrapped in a thick scarf and determination. "Hey, girls. I'm hunting for succulents today. And ceramic pots. Something small but not too boring. You know, for the café window."

"We just got a few new ones in," I said, gesturing toward the back shelf. "The blue-glazed ones would match your café walls."

Maggie wandered over with a thoughtful nod, already sizing up each pot like it had to interview for the job. Poppy leaned toward me and murmured, "Between the Reverend, the mayor's assistant, and now Maggie, this shop's had more foot traffic than a street fair — and it's not even ten yet."

I gave her a wry smile. "Better than silence. Especially with all these invoices we have to pay."

She nodded once, fingers still tapping away at her keyboard.

"Shipment in?" Poppy asked without looking up.

"Yep, just got here." I set a bulky cardboard box on the counter.

"Charlene's got us working overtime with her gala requests. I swear she thinks we have magical, self-arranging flowers."

Poppy snorted, finally glancing up. "One of these days, I'm going to tell her that 'floral magic' has limits."

I smirked. "Good luck with that. Maybe you can tell her the flowers aren't wizards."

She let out a laugh before grabbing a pair of scissors. Together, we began unboxing the shipment, working in that easy rhythm we'd perfected over years of arranging, sorting, and preparing blooms.

The usual mix of orchids, roses, and peonies spilled from their protective wrapping, vibrant and fragrant. The morning light filtering through the shop's front window cast a golden hue over everything, making it feel — if only for a moment — like just another ordinary day.

Then my fingers stilled.

Something was… off.

The flower in my grasp didn't belong. Its deep purple petals curled at the edges like claws, and its waxy leaves gleamed under the shop lights with an eerie sheen. A sharp, bitter scent cut through the usual floral sweetness, distinct and unmistakable.

A chill crept up my spine.

"Poppy," I murmured, my voice quieter than I intended. "Look at this."

Poppy leaned in, her nose wrinkling. "Whoa. What is that?"

I set it down carefully. "Wolfsbane."

Poppy took a quick step back. "As in the poisonous kind?"

I nodded, scanning the invoice with a frown. "It wasn't on the order list."

Poppy grabbed the page and skimmed it. "Roses, orchids, peonies… nope. No wolfsbane."

Before I could respond, the bell above the shop's front door jingled, and Scott stepped inside, fresh from school drop-off. His easy demeanor shifted the second he saw our faces. "What's with the looks?"

Poppy gestured to the counter. "Someone slipped wolfsbane into our shipment."

Scott frowned, stepping closer. "That stuff's dangerous. Why would a flower shop get a delivery of poison?"

Before I could even begin to form an answer, the bell jingled again, and Dolly, our ever-cheerful assistant, swept inside carrying a tray of coffee.

"Fuel for the floral warriors!" she declared, setting the cups down. But her grin faded when she noticed the tension in the room. "Uh… did I miss something? Y'all look like you just found a dead mouse in the roses."

Poppy motioned to the unsettling bloom. "Not a mouse. Just wolfsbane."

Dolly's eyes widened. "Like the murder-mystery flower? Why is that here?"

"That's what we're trying to figure out," Poppy muttered.

Scott folded his arms. "Could it be a mistake? Maybe someone at the greenhouse misread a label?"

I shook my head. "It doesn't feel like an accident."

Dolly took a cautious step back. "This… isn't bad bad, right? We're not, like, in trouble?"

I didn't answer right away, letting the silence settle between us.

Scott finally exhaled, rubbing the back of his neck. "Well, whatever this is, you should be careful. I don't like the idea of someone messing with your shipments — especially not with something this toxic."

I nodded, my gaze locked on the dark petals.

Poppy crossed her arms. "So… what do we do?"

A slow, uneasy feeling settled in my chest. Something wasn't adding up.

"We pay attention," I said firmly. "Because I think this is just the beginning."

The shop, usually filled with warmth and beauty, suddenly felt heavier — like the air itself was holding its breath.

The wolfsbane sat there, dark and ominous, a message in petals.

And whoever sent it... wanted us to know.

Just as Scott stepped out, the bell jingled again.

Mrs. Bosley walked in with her usual quiet grace, bundled in a pale blue coat and soft floral scarf. Her presence always brought a kind of nostalgia—like cinnamon cookies and stories you only half remembered.

"Good morning, dears," she said gently. "I was hoping I could pick up a bouquet of fresh-cut daisies?"

Poppy blinked, her expression softening immediately. "Of course, Mrs. Bosley. Is it a special occasion?"

She smiled wistfully. "It's my mother's birthday today. She adored daisies. I thought I'd take a bouquet to lay by her graveside."

Dolly gave a little "awww" from behind the counter before skipping over to help Maggie, still browsing at potted succulents. Mrs. Bosley stepped closer to the register, waiting patiently as the shop returned to its regular rhythm.

Poppy and I exchanged a quiet look — our previous tension lingering beneath the surface.

"Let's get those daisies," I said, motioning toward the back room.

We slipped behind the curtain, the weight of the morning still hanging heavy in the air, now softened just slightly by a simple act of remembrance.

Sometimes in Bloomwood, even grief bloomed gently — right alongside secrets and poison.

And in a flower shop like ours, you had to learn how to make space for both.

Chapter 2

Coffee Run at Maggie's

I was just there for coffee.

One large house blend, two muffins, and about five minutes of pretending I didn't overhear anything I wasn't supposed to. That was the plan. But as always in Bloomwood, things

THORNE SISTERS COZY MYSTERY: PETALS, POISON, AND PERIL

didn't go according to plan.

The scent of cinnamon and freshly brewed coffee wrapped around me the second I stepped into Maggie's Café. It was early — the kind of gray morning where the sky couldn't decide if it wanted to rain or stay broody and dramatic. I was still half-asleep, my brain clinging to the hope that caffeine would solve all my problems.

I nodded at the couple in the corner booth and took my place in line, one eye on the clock and the other on the pastry case.

That's when Charles Dixon

walked in.

Even without his usual entourage of smugness, he made an entrance — coat crisp, scarf perfectly knotted, and the sort of expression that made it clear he thought the world should part like the sea when he walked into a room. He made a beeline for the counter where Margo stood polishing a tray, and I instinctively shrank behind a hanging fern near the register.

Not intentionally eavesdropping. Just… strategically located. "Morning, Maggie," he said, his tone lighter than the tension in his shoulders. "The usual. And make the eggs a little less runny this time?" Maggie smiled, but it didn't reach her eyes. "Sure thing, Charles. Anything for my favorite investor."

Investor?

I blinked, surprised. That was news. I'd never heard her mention anything about having a silent partner — especially not *that* one.

She poured his coffee with steady hands, but her voice had a curious edge when she asked, "Big night tonight, huh? The mayor's gala?"

Charles chuckled. "Should be quite the event."

There was a pause. A beat too long. I peeked from behind the fern.

"If you've got an extra ticket," Margo said casually, "I wouldn't mind joining you. Might be good for people to see us together. Show the café's doing well."

Charles froze mid-sip.

"Maggie, you don't belong at that kind of event," he said with a laugh that felt more like a slap. "Stay here. Make some money. That's how you protect our investment."

I winced.

Maggie did, too — but hers came with fire.

"So I'm good enough to run the café, but not stand beside you at a gala?"

He waved it off. "This isn't personal."

"Isn't it?" she shot back. "You told me once this place was *ours*. We were in this together."

He pushed his plate away. "It *is* ours. But your place is here, not playing politics."

The café had gone quiet. Even the espresso machine seemed to hold its breath.

"I can't believe you," she said, her voice rising. "You think just because you wrote a check, you get to decide who belongs where?"

"Maggie—"

"Don't start this here," he warned.

But she already had.

"You don't want me at the gala because you don't want people to know you've been laundering your political mess through this café!"

My jaw dropped slightly. Even Bessie Jenkins put down her crossword.

Charles's face turned a shade darker. "Keep your voice down."

"Why? So you can control the narrative like you always do?"

He turned and stormed toward

the door.

Maggie's final words followed him like a dagger.

"I *hate* you, Charles Dixon!"

The bell over the door jingled. And then he was gone.

I stood rooted in place, blinking, heart thudding in my ears. Maggie didn't look my way. She just turned and wiped down the counter like she hadn't just publicly yelled at a man.

As I picked up my coffee from the end of the bar, she finally glanced at me and offered a smile so brittle I thought it might crack.

I smiled back, trying to look normal.

"Morning," she said evenly.

"Morning," I replied, though my voice came out higher than intended.

Then I walked out into the chilly Bloomwood morning, the coffee forgotten in my hand, and the memory of her words echoing in my mind.

I hate you, Charles Dixon.

And that's when I knew.

The gala was going to be anything but festive.

Chapter 3

A Gala to Remember

The grand ballroom of the Bloomwood Hotel gleamed like a polished gemstone, the golden light from countless chandeliers reflecting off the marble floors. Elegantly dressed guests moved in fluid waves, glasses of champagne glistening in their hands as murmured conversations and polite laughter filled the air. Beneath it all, the familiar fragrance of our floral arrangements — roses, lilies, and exotic orchids — layered over the crisp scent of starched linens and expensive perfume.

I took a slow breath, letting my gaze sweep across the room. The towering centerpieces stood like art installations, the rich hues of deep magenta orchids, ivory roses, and feathery greenery weaving together in perfect harmony. *Blossom & Thorne* had outdone itself tonight.

Beside me, Poppy crossed her arms, her dark eyes flickering toward the mayor's table. "Let's just hope Charlene actually acknowledges us in her speech. You know she loves taking credit for things she didn't lift a finger for."

I smirked, smoothing the midnight-blue satin of my gown. "I'd settle for her not butchering our shop's name this time."

As if summoned by our words, Mayor Charlene Whitfield glided toward us, a vision of calculated poise in an emerald gown. Her assistant, Kenneth Marshall, hovered just behind her, as he always did, whispering whatever bits of information helped keep her ahead of the game.

"Ladies," Charlene greeted, extending a perfectly manicured hand. "Your arrangements are absolutely stunning. You've truly transformed the space."

I returned the smile, the one I had mastered over years of business dealings, polite but unreadable. "Thank you, Mayor Whitfield. We're glad you're pleased."

Poppy, ever less inclined toward diplomatic niceties, gave a curt nod. "Glad they meet your expectations."

Charlene's smile faltered just a fraction, but she recovered quickly. Kenneth leaned in and whispered something in her ear, and her expression hardened. Whatever it was, she didn't share. Instead, she nodded once and turned on her heel.

"Excuse me," she said smoothly. "I see Charles Dixon has arrived, and I need to have a word with him."

Poppy arched a brow as we both watched Charlene make a beeline for Dixon. "What's the over-under on her speech including a jab at him?"

I adjusted a stray orchid in the nearest arrangement. "Low-hanging fruit. She can't resist."

Dixon stood near the buffet table, his broad shoulders stiff, whiskey glass in hand. He was as commanding a presence as Charlene, but where she was all polish and control, he was rough edges and unfiltered opinions. The two of them had been locked in a political cold war for months, and I had a feeling we were about to see the latest battle unfold.

The moment they faced each other, the shift in the air was immediate. The cordial masks cracked, and tension rolled off them in waves.

"You think you're untouchable, Charlene," Dixon said, his voice gravelly and thick with barely restrained anger. "But I have the proof.

I'll expose you for what you really are, and this whole town will see it."

Charlene's response was quieter, more measured. Her eyes, sharp as a blade, held no trace of fear — only warning. Whatever she said, it was lost in the hum of the ballroom, but her body language spoke volumes.

The mayor let out a deep sigh, "I wish I could just get rid of him," she said to Kenneth. Then, with a sharp turn, she walked away, Kenneth following closely behind her, leaving Dixon standing there, his fingers clenched around his glass.

Poppy leaned in, voice low. "Did you hear that? Proof of what?"

I shrugged, keeping my tone even despite my own curiosity. "Probably just more political mudslinging. They've been circling each other for months."

"Still," Poppy muttered, eyes locked on Dixon, "he didn't sound like he was bluffing."

The incident didn't go unnoticed. The murmur of speculation wove through the crowd, subtle but persistent. But the champagne kept flowing, the music played on, and the night pressed forward as if nothing had happened.

"Your arrangements are breathtaking," a woman in a deep violet gown gushed as she passed us. "They bring such elegance to the evening."

Poppy and I exchanged a knowing look, a silent agreement to push aside whatever had just unfolded between the mayor and Dixon. For now, this was our moment—to bask in the success of our work, to accept the well-earned compliments.

Still, a sliver of unease curled at the edges of my mind.

The Bloomwood Civic Hall shimmered under a sea of golden twinkle lights, laughter floating like champagne bubbles in the air. But beneath the elegance of the mayor's gala, secrets pulsed just beneath the surface.

I was near the refreshment table, fiddling with my glass of sparkling cider, when I spotted them, Reverend Michael Robinson and Charles Dixon, standing just beyond the reach of the string lights, half-shadowed near the tall arched windows. Their posture was stiff. The smiles were gone.

I stepped just close enough to pretend I was inspecting the cheese display. My ears, however, were fully tuned in.

"You didn't have to come, Charles," Reverend Robinson said, voice low and carefully even. "Not sure the Lord needs your presence at this particular gathering."

Dixon let out a humorless chuckle. "I didn't come to be seen, Reverend. I came to make something right."

"Now there's a phrase I've heard before," Robinson replied, folding his hands in front of him. "Usually right after a mess is made."

Dixon's jaw twitched. "I know I made mistakes. But the church was never supposed to be part of it."

"Wasn't it?" The Reverend tilted his head. "That community grant you twisted into a campaign fund? That was meant to build homes, not headlines."

"I panicked," Dixon said, voice cracking just slightly. "But I never forgot what I owed."

Robinson was silent, watching him with unreadable eyes.

"I left something for the church," Dixon added, softer now. "It's in my will. Enough to restore the youth center... maybe expand the pantry."

Michael blinked slowly. "A gift doesn't erase the past, Charles."

"I'm not asking you to erase anything." Dixon stepped a little closer, lowering his voice. "I'm asking you to believe that — for once — I'm trying to do the right thing."

Reverend Robinson's expression softened. Only a little. "Intentions matter less than consistency."

Dixon gave a faint nod. "I don't have much time to be consistent."
A beat of silence stretched between them, heavy with meaning.

Finally, Michael extended a hand. "Then start here. Start now."
Dixon took it, though his grip trembled.

And just like that, the moment passed. They pulled apart, and Dixon disappeared back into the crowd, leaving Reverend Robinson alone under the soft light.

From across the room, I saw the Reverend close his eyes, like he was offering up a silent prayer — or maybe a warning to the heavens.

Whatever their past was, it hadn't been buried.

And from the look on Reverend Robinson's face, I wasn't sure it ever would be.

As the night wore on, the ballroom slowly emptying as guests trickled out into the crisp evening air.

Near the buffet table, Dixon was s deep in another conversation with a small group, his laugh deep and jovial. Yet even as he laughed, I couldn't shake the memory of the venom in his voice earlier.

I have the proof. I'll expose you.

Those weren't empty words. They carried weight. And whatever Charles Dixon knew, it was enough to rattle Mayor Charlene Whitfield, even if only for a moment.

Poppy and I gathered our things, stepping outside into the night. The sky above Bloomwood was clear, stars glittering like scattered diamonds. I inhaled deeply, the cool air washing away the heaviness of the ballroom.

"Another successful event in the books," I said, my voice light despite the thoughts stirring in my mind.

Poppy crossed her arms against the chill, her gaze flickering back toward the glowing windows of the hotel. "Maybe," she murmured. "But I have a feeling we haven't heard the last of tonight."

I studied her for a moment. "Still thinking about Dixon?"

She nodded, her expression tight. "I don't think he's bluffing, Iris. He knows something—and whatever it is, it's dangerous."

I didn't respond right away. Instead, I let the silence stretch between us as we walked back toward the shop, our heels clicking softly against the pavement.

Somewhere in the shadows of Bloomwood, a storm was brewing. We just didn't know it yet.

Chapter 4

Death Among the Roses

Morning sunlight streamed through the wide windows of *Blossom & Thorne*, turning the shop into a canvas of warm gold. The scent of fresh-cut roses, lavender, and eucalyptus swirled in the air, mixing with the soft melody of classical music playing from the old radio near the register.

I stood by a display of lilies, adjusting their stems so that each bloom caught the light just right. Floristry was as much about precision as it was about beauty, and in moments like this, the shop felt like the peaceful refuge it had always been — at least until reality interrupted.

The phone rang sharply, slicing through the calm.

Poppy, who had been behind the counter sorting ribbons, reached for the receiver. "Blossom & Thorne, this is Poppy."

I barely paid attention at first, but then her body stiffened.

Her fingers tightened around the receiver, her face draining of color. "Oh no," she whispered. "That's... terrible."

My heart clenched. I knew that tone.

"Poppy?" I took a step toward her, my voice careful but firm. "What is it?"

She slowly lowered the phone, almost as if it had burned her. When she finally turned to face me, her expression sent a chill through my bones.

"It's Charles Dixon," she said, her voice unsteady. "He was found dead this morning… poisoned."

The warmth of the morning suddenly felt distant, the golden sunlight paling under the weight of her words.

"Poisoned?" I repeated, my mind already racing ahead to what that could mean. "How?"

"The police think it was wolfsbane," Poppy said, and her eyes locked onto mine, the fear behind them unmistakable. "Iris… what if—"

The shop's front bell jingled, cutting off her thought.

We both turned as two uniformed officers stepped inside. Leading them was a woman in a sharply tailored suit, her presence commanding even in the midst of our shop's usual warmth. Her gaze swept the room, precise and calculating, before landing on us.

"Ms. Thorne and Ms. Thorne?" she asked, her voice steady and authoritative. "I'm Detective Jennifer Tyler with the Bloomwood Police Department. I need to ask you a few questions about Charles Dixon."

I felt my throat tighten, but I pushed down the wave of unease and stepped forward. "Of course, Detective. We just heard about… what happened."

Tyler gave a curt nod. "Mr. Dixon was poisoned by wolfsbane, and preliminary evidence traces the source back to your shop."

"What?" Poppy exclaimed, her voice pitching higher. "That's impossible! We'd never sell something so dangerous."

Tyler reached into her bag and pulled out a small plastic evidence bag. Inside, nestled against the clear plastic, was a fragment of a dark purple flower—its jagged petals still eerily vibrant.

"This was found in Mr. Dixon's wineglass at his home," Tyler continued. "Lab results confirm it's wolfsbane—the same species you reported receiving in your recent shipment."

The room tilted for a moment, or maybe it was just me. The memory of the sinister plant flashed vividly in my mind, its unnatural presence among our usual flowers.

"We didn't use it for anything," I said quickly. "We didn't even order it!

It was a mistake, something we set aside as soon as we saw it."

Tyler's sharp gaze locked onto mine. "Can anyone corroborate that?"

"Our assistant, Dolly," Poppy said. "She saw it too. We were all surprised when it showed up in the shipment."

Tyler made a note in her small, leather-bound notebook, her pen moving with crisp efficiency. "Did anyone else have access to the wolfsbane after it arrived?"

I hesitated, my mind flipping through the past few days. Who had been near the workroom? Who had come into our space without a second thought?

"Kenneth Marshall," I said suddenly.

Tyler's brow arched slightly. "The mayor's assistant?"

I nodded. "He came by the shop the day before the gala. He said he was checking on the arrangements. He was near the workroom... but we didn't think much of it at the time."

Poppy chewed her lip, eyes narrowing. "Now that I think about it, he was lingering back there longer than necessary."

Tyler's expression remained unreadable, but I didn't miss the way her grip on her notebook tightened slightly.

"I'll need the names of everyone who visited your shop in the past week," she said, "as well as any employees who might have handled the plant."

I nodded, keeping my voice steady even as my stomach twisted into knots. "Of course, Detective. But you have to believe us—we would never use something like that."

Tyler's gaze softened, just a fraction. "I believe you," she admitted.

"But that doesn't change the fact that the wolfsbane came from here. If someone used your shop to commit murder, you're already tied to this case."

The weight of her words settled over me like an anchor.

With a final glance around the shop, Tyler and the officers turned to leave, the shop bell jingling again in their wake. The sound felt heavier than before, less like the welcoming chime it usually was and more like the tolling of a warning bell.

For a long moment, neither Poppy nor I spoke.

Then, finally, Poppy exhaled, shaking her head. "This is bad," she whispered. "If we don't figure out who did this, our shop—our reputation—everything we've worked for could be ruined."

I took a slow, deliberate breath. My sister wasn't wrong.

"We'll clear our name," I said, my voice firmer than I felt. "Someone used *Blossom & Thorne* to cover their tracks, and we're going to find out who—and why."

Determination settled in my chest, anchoring me in a way I hadn't expected.

I had just slid the deadbolt into place when the bell above the front door jingled, making me jump. It was after closing, and the shop was supposed to be locked tight. I turned around, ready to remind whoever it was about our hours — only to see Mrs. Bosley bustling in like a woman with a purpose, her tote bag bulging with paperback romances and half-eaten licorice sticks poking out like stubborn weeds.

"Girls, I meant to say something earlier, but you know how my mind works," she said, fluttering her fingers as her eyes bounced between Poppy and me. "Last night, I was up refilling my hummingbird feeders—don't ask, Harold insists the birds prefer moonlight—and I saw someone standing outside your shop. Just standing there. Not moving. Just... watching."

The hairs on the back of my neck stood up. Watching? At that hour? The street would've been quiet—empty, even. And someone had been lurking?

Poppy stepped forward, arms crossing. "Watching how? Like casing the place?"

Mrs. Bosley shrugged, clearly delighted by the intrigue she was creating. "Couldn't make out the face. Hoodie up. Tall. Male, I think. Gave me the willies, that's for sure. But when I opened the window to get a better look, he turned and walked off toward Main Street." She lowered her voice, leaning in. "Looked a lot like that Kenneth fellow. You know, the professor-turned-plant-whisperer? Always seemed too slick to me. Like someone playing a part."

I met Poppy's gaze, and the silent exchange said everything. My pulse skipped, then quickened. That wasn't just an offhand remark. It was a puzzle piece. The wolfsbane hadn't just arrived tucked into our shipment. Someone had placed it. Chosen it. Left it where we'd find it.

And now, for the first time, I had a name attached to that possibility. Kenneth. Too knowledgeable. Too convenient. Too perfect.

Too suspicious.

The wolfsbane sat in the back of the shop, its dark petals seeming to mock us. Whoever had placed it in that shipment, whoever had slipped it into Dixon's wine glass, had left a trail—one we needed to follow.

Because whether we liked it or not, we weren't just florists anymore.

We were part of this mystery. And if we didn't solve it, we'd be the next ones with a target on our backs.

Chapter 5

Thornes of Suspicion

The usual comforting scent of *Blossom & Thorne* — roses, lilies, and lavender — felt oddly oppressive today, pressing in around me like a weighted blanket I couldn't throw off. Normally, the back workroom was a place of calm creativity, where arrangements came together like quiet poetry under our hands.

But today, even the soft golden light filtering through the window felt accusatory.

I sat at the work table, pen tapping rhythmically against the blank page of my notebook — a nervous habit I hadn't noticed until now. Scattered across the table were receipts, order slips, and a smear of yellow pollen. None of it helped settle the knot forming in my stomach.

Across from me, Poppy leaned forward, arms crossed, staring at the notepad like it owed her an explanation.

"We need to make a list," I said finally, breaking the silence. "Everyone who came into the shop the morning the wolfsbane arrived."

Poppy sighed, picking up a pen and clicking it with more force than necessary. "It wasn't exactly Black Friday. Most people called in their orders or picked up curbside."

"Still," I said, already scribbling the first name, "someone might've had a chance to slip it in."

Dolly.

"She was working that morning.

She helped unload the delivery and saw us set the wolfsbane aside."

Poppy nodded. "Right. And next... Mrs. Bosley?"

I paused mid-scribble, blinking. "Mrs. Bosley?"

Poppy gave me a helpless shrug. "She came in to pick up that bouquet of daisies for her mother's gravesite. Remember?"

I smiled despite myself. "You think sweet Mrs. Bosley slipped us a murder flower between talking about homemade jam and weather updates?"

Poppy snorted. "The woman once gave me a tin of cookies and told me it was a family recipe passed down by her great-aunt who eloped with a moonshiner. I wouldn't put anything past her."

I giggled as I jotted down her name—half out of habit, half because we'd promised to be thorough.

Maggie Bishop went down next.

"She was shopping for succulents," I said. "Didn't she stop by that morning asking about new ceramic pots?"

Poppy rolled her eyes. "Yes, and complained about how the town was wasting money on 'glitter and lights' while her café barely made rent."

"She wasn't thrilled about the gala or Charles either, I heard her arguing with him and yell that she hated him the morning of the gala at the cafe," I added, underlining her name twice. "She's got history with Charles, and she's not subtle about it."

Poppy tapped the pen against her chin. "If she wanted to make a statement, slipping wolfsbane into our shop wouldn't exactly be on-brand… for a cafe, but it would be dramatic."

I jotted a side note: *Financial tension, outspoken. Strong opinions.*

"Okay," I continued.
"Next—Reverend Michael Robinson."

Poppy's brow lifted. "Reverend Robinson? You really think the Reverend—?"

I shrugged. "He came in that morning, remember? Picked up a sympathy arrangement for the Maxwell family funeral."

"And he was oddly quiet," Poppy said, eyes narrowing. "Didn't stay to chat, which is weird for him. He usually gives us a whole sermon with his pick-up."

"I also saw him later that day," I added slowly. "In the cemetery talking to Maggie."

Poppy's eyes widened. "What?"

"They were arguing. Well — talking, but it didn't look friendly. He told her something like, 'The past only stays buried if you let it.'"

Poppy leaned forward. "Now that's cryptic."

I wrote his name with a star beside it. Reverend Michael Robinson.

And finally…

Kenneth Marshall.

"The most obvious," I murmured. "The Mayor's assistant. He came in the day before the gala and was way too interested in the workroom."

Poppy nodded. "He kept asking questions about the arrangements. And I caught him staring at the delivery box we'd used to isolate the wolfsbane."

"Did he touch it?"

"I don't think so," she said, "but he was definitely lingering longer than he needed to."

I underlined his name three times. "Kenneth had motive, access, and knowledge. He's at the top of the list."

Just then, the back door creaked open, and Dolly swept in, juggling a bundle of receipts in one hand and a half-melted iced coffee in the other. The faint scent of vanilla syrup followed her in like a ghost.

"Hey, ladies," she chirped. "What's with the murder board?"

"We're making a list," I said. "People who were in the shop the morning the wolfsbane came in."

Dolly's brows rose. "Oooh. Am I on it?"

"You're at the top," Poppy said dryly.

Dolly gasped with mock horror. "How dare you? I only poison people with baked goods and charm."

Poppy snorted. "We're just covering all bases. Do you remember Kenneth Marshall that day?"

Dolly nodded quickly. "He gave me the creeps. Kept peeking into the back like he was looking for something."

I jotted her memory down. "Okay, that confirms it."

Dolly took a seat on the stool near the wall, sipping her coffee. "Y'all better be careful. If someone's playing dirty with your flowers, they might not stop at petals."

Her words lingered longer than I wanted them to.

I looked down at the list. Five names. Five possibilities. One dead man. And a poisonous bloom no one had asked for.

This wasn't an accident.

The wolfsbane was deliberate. And someone—maybe someone we trusted—had left it there for a reason.

I looked up at Poppy. "Next step?"

She didn't hesitate. "We start watching them. All of them."

And just like that, the hunt was on.

Chapter 6

Glitter, Grudges, and Revelations

Poppy and I walked side by side down Bloomwood's main street, and the whole town looked like it had been caught in a glittery whirlwind. Twinkle lights were going up over every storefront, casting warm reflections in freshly polished windows. The scent of fresh paint lingered outside Maggie's Café, like someone had just finished brushing the trim ten minutes ago.

A brand-new chalkboard sign stood proudly out front in swirly cursive:

"Try Our Gala-Blend Spiced Latte!"

I had to admit—it smelled good. Even if the name was trying a little too hard.

Just as we passed the café, Maggie herself came out with a steaming tray of drinks for her outdoor tables. She was dressed in her usual mix of black and bold floral prints, her silver hair swept into a no-nonsense twist.

"Morning," she called, then added with a dramatic sigh, "Enjoy the lights while they last. Town council blew half the budget on those twinkly things while half of us are still patching cracked sidewalks."

"Everything looks lovely, Maggie," Poppy offered, ever the diplomat.

Maggie rolled her eyes. "Lovely doesn't pay the bills. Charlene's zoning changes redirected foot traffic straight past my café. Meanwhile, Dixon promised me he'd raise hell at the next meeting and then — poof — nothing."

Her voice dropped, bitter. "Maybe someone should've shut him up before he ruined more lives."

I blinked at her, unsure if she meant it or if it was just Maggie being Maggie. Either way, I mentally filed her comment under *offhand remarks that sound like gossip but feel like warnings.* Bloomwood was full of them.

"Speaking of parties," she continued, tipping her chin toward the civic center, "I heard the gala's seating arrangement nearly caused a fistfight. If Charlene seats Dixon's niece next to the Chamber of Commerce rep again, there won't be enough wine in town to keep it civil."

She gave us a curt wave and turned back inside, the bell above her café door jingling softly.

Across the street, Mr. Chen was wobbling on a ladder outside the hardware store, a bucket of gold balloons swaying dangerously in the wind. He waved with one hand, grumbling with the other.

"Let's hope all this fuss is worth it. Charlene's been tightening purse strings all year, and now she wants a parade? Hmph."

Typical Mr. Chen—always half-helpful, half-grumbling.

Farther down, June Applegate

was knee-deep in glitter and feathered masks, fussing with her boutique window like she was designing for a Paris runway.

"I just love this kind of thing," she gushed to Poppy. "Say what you want about Charlene, she knows how to put on a party. Though between you and me, the council's still fuming over those budget cuts. Half of them are only showing up tonight to drink and glare."

Poppy chuckled, but I filed that one too.

Because if there's one thing I've learned from living in Bloomwood, it's this:

When you mix glitter with grudges, someone always ends up sweeping up more than confetti.

Back at the apartment above *Blossom & Thorne*, our cozy living room no longer resembled a home. It looked more like a scene from a quirky detective drama—part amateur sleuth headquarters, part controlled chaos.

Stacks of papers, open laptops, and half-drunk mugs of cold coffee cluttered every surface. The coffee table was buried in scribbled notes, highlighted articles, and a large photo of Charles Dixon, his stern eyes frozen in time, watching over us like a ghost who still had something to say.

The comforting scent of Poppy's lavender sachet mingled with the harsher aroma of burned coffee and stress.

I tapped Dixon's photo with my pen. "We need to figure out why he was such a threat to Charlene. What was he planning to expose?"

Poppy, cross-legged on the couch with her laptop glowing in her lap, muttered, "He was always ranting about corruption in Charlene's administration, but it was vague—bluster, mostly. Maybe there's something buried in his old posts."

She stopped scrolling, eyes narrowing. "Wait—check this out. Two days before the gala, he posted: *'The truth will come out. Bloomwood deserves better leadership.'*"

I leaned over her shoulder. "Look at the comments. People asked for proof, and he replied, *'Soon, everyone will see for themselves.'*"

Our eyes met. That quiet chill again.

Dixon had been planning something. Something big.

I reached for a stack of news clippings until one headline practically jumped off the page:

"**Dixon Accuses Mayor Whitfield of Misappropriating Funds**."

"Listen to this," I read. "'*Dixon claims Mayor Charlene Whitfield funneled city funds through a shell company for personal gain. The investigation stalled due to insufficient evidence.*'"

Poppy crossed her arms. "What if he finally found the evidence?"

I nodded slowly, the thought settling like a stone in my gut. "Then someone had a very good reason to keep him quiet."

Poppy's voice dropped, a dry smile tugging at the corner of her mouth. "And now we're Bloomwood's very own Nancy Drews... with a floral license."

I smirked. "Speak for yourself. I was always more of a Trixie Belden girl."

She laughed. "Please. You live for a well-labeled file folder and a mystery to solve."

"Fair," I admitted, reaching for another stack of articles. "But I draw the line at matching trench coats."

A sound startled us — the front door flying open.

Phillip and Violet tumbled inside, followed by Scott, who stopped dead in the doorway when he saw the chaos.

Phillip blinked. "Uh… Mom? What is this?"

Violet's gasp was practically theatrical. "Are you two spies now?"

Poppy grinned. "Something like that."

Scott raised an eyebrow. "I thought you two were running a flower shop, not solving crimes."

"Desperate times," I replied, moving a stack of old receipts so Phillip could set down his school folder.

Scott gave a low chuckle but his

face quickly sobered. "I get it. I do. But if someone killed Dixon to keep him quiet, you don't want to end up next on their list."

Poppy shrugged. "We're just researching public records. Nothing illegal."

Scott didn't look convinced. "Promise me you won't do anything reckless."

"Define reckless," Poppy said with a grin.

Scott sighed and turned to herd the kids.

"Okay, but can you clear a spot

on the couch soon?" Phillip asked, stepping carefully over a file folder. "I miss sitting down."

Violet crossed her arms. "If this is a detective agency, I want to be a secret agent."

"You're hired," Poppy said. "Welcome to the team, Agent Violet."

Scott laughed and scooped her up. "Alright, Agent Violet, mission bedtime begins now."

The hallway echoed with giggles as they disappeared.

Then the front door creaked again.

Dolly walked in, uncharacteristically quiet. Her sparkly earrings still jingled, but her usual pep had dulled. In her hand was a worn manila folder, its edges rumpled.

"You're gonna want to see this," she said, setting it down on the coffee table.

Poppy opened it. The air left the room.

Bribery. Embezzlement. Kickbacks.

"Kenneth Marshall did time Upstate," I said, flipping through the documents. "He was accused of taking kickbacks. Charges dropped, but his name never recovered."

"And guess who hired him next?" Dolly said. "Charlene."

Poppy shook her head. "So he owes her. Big time."

"Bigger than you know," Dolly said. "Someone overheard him at the gala, saying Dixon was going to 'ruin everything' and had to be stopped."

I swallowed hard. "If Dixon had evidence and Kenneth was in too deep…"

Poppy's voice was tight. "Then we're not imagining things. Someone killed him. And we're not safe."

"Dolly where did you get this file and intel on Kenneth?"

"Sorry, girls I can't divulge my source. Let's just say I have a friend who is a private detective, and they wanted to help pro bono when I told them about our situation over here."

A soft ding broke the silence. Poppy checked her phone and blinked.

"Bloomwood Gazette," she murmured. Then her voice caught. "Headline reads: *'Dixon's Final Investigation: Was He About to Uncover Political Corruption?'*"

I read the article over her shoulder: *"Friends say Dixon was preparing a bombshell revelation, set to shake Bloomwood's political landscape."*

The silence between us was thick with implication.

"If Charlene and Kenneth were willing to kill to keep things buried..." I said, "they won't stop now."

Poppy nodded slowly. "Then we don't stop either."

We turned back to our makeshift crime board. The threads of Bloomwood's secrets were unraveling—and we weren't just arranging bouquets anymore.

We were hunting a killer.

And the list of suspects was still growing.

Chapter 7

A Poisonous Lead

The night air was sharp against my skin, the scent of damp leaves and distant chimney smoke curling through the quiet streets of Bloomwood. Poppy and I walked briskly down the cobblestone path toward the municipal building, our breath forming small clouds in the cold. The tension in my jaw matched the determined rhythm of our footsteps.

"He won't expect us to confront him," I murmured, my fingers tightening around the strap of my bag. "We need to catch him off guard."

Poppy clutched her leather satchel closer, her posture stiff. "If he's hiding something, we'll know."

The municipal building loomed ahead, its concrete facade washed in the sterile glow of fluorescent lighting. Inside, the air was thick with the scent of old paper and cleaning solution. The overhead lights buzzed faintly, casting long shadows across the tiled floor.

Across the room, Kenneth Marshall sat hunched over a stack of documents, his rolled-up sleeves exposing the silver glint of his watch. He didn't notice us until I spoke.

"Mr. Marshall," I said, keeping my voice calm but firm. "We need to talk."

Kenneth's head snapped up. For a split second, surprise flickered across his face, quickly replaced by a smooth, practiced smile. "The Thorne sisters," he said, leaning back in his chair. "What can I do for you?"

Poppy wasted no time. "It's about Charles Dixon," she said, her voice sharp. "And the wolfsbane that came through our shop."

Kenneth blinked, his confident mask slipping for just a moment. His fingers laced together on the desk as he exhaled slowly. "I don't see what that has to do with me."

I folded my arms. "You were in our shop the day before the gala. You had access to the flowers, including the wolfsbane. And now Dixon is dead — poisoned by it."

He let out a forced chuckle, shaking his head. "That's quite the accusation." He leaned forward slightly. "I was there to check on the arrangements for the mayor. If you're looking for someone to blame, I suggest you look elsewhere."

Poppy tilted her head, her eyes narrowing. "You seem to know a lot about the wolfsbane," she said pointedly. "More than you should."

For a second, Kenneth's face froze, his carefully constructed composure cracking. "What's that supposed to mean?" he snapped, standing abruptly.

I stepped forward, keeping my voice measured. "You just confirmed the wolfsbane was in our shop. That detail hasn't been made public."

His eyes widened ever so slightly before he covered his reaction with a scoff. He grabbed his coat in a flurry of movement. "You're twisting my words," he muttered. "I don't have time for this nonsense."

He stormed past us, his polished shoes clicking against the tile.

Poppy exhaled sharply. "Did you see that? He knows something."

I nodded, already moving toward the exit. "Let's find out what."

The cold night wrapped around us as we followed Kenneth through the quiet streets. His hurried steps and nervous glances over his shoulder told us everything we needed to know — he wasn't just irritated. He was rattled.

We kept a safe distance, sticking to the shadows as the scent of wet pavement and woodsmoke clung to the crisp air. The streetlamps cast long, distorted shadows as Kenneth moved briskly ahead, his shoulders hunched, weighed down by whatever secrets he was keeping.

Then, he suddenly veered down a narrow alley.

Poppy and I exchanged a glance before pressing ourselves against the rough brick wall, peering around the corner.

Kenneth wasn't alone.

A man stood at the other end of the alley, his heavy coat obscuring his frame, a cap pulled low over his face. Even from here, something about him felt... deliberate. Like he wasn't just another late-night passerby.

Kenneth gestured animatedly, his hands slicing through the air as he spoke. The stranger remained still, nodding occasionally, exuding an eerie calm. Their voices were too low for us to hear, but the tension between them was unmistakable.

Then, Kenneth reached into his coat and pulled out a thick envelope.

Poppy tensed beside me. "What's in there?" she whispered. "Money? Documents?"

I barely breathed. "Whatever it is, it's shady."

The stranger took the envelope without hesitation, slipping it into his coat pocket before turning and disappearing into the shadows.

Kenneth lingered for a moment, scanning the alley as if ensuring he hadn't been seen. Then, he turned and walked briskly back the way he'd come.

Poppy and I shrank deeper into the shadows as he passed, his jaw clenched, his face taut with worry. The faint scent of cologne and damp city air clung to his wake.

Only when he was out of sight did Poppy exhale. "That wasn't just a friendly chat. He's covering something up."

I nodded slowly. "And now we know he's not acting alone."

Poppy glanced toward the alley's darkened end. "What do we do now?"

I tightened my scarf against the cold, my mind already spinning. "We follow the money — or whatever was in that envelope. Kenneth just gave us our next lead."

We stepped away from the alley, our breath still visible in the cold night air. The deeper we dug, the more dangerous this was becoming. But stopping now? That wasn't an option.

The truth was just within reach.

And we weren't going to let it slip away.

Chapter 8

Ledger and Warning

I leaned back in my chair, rubbing my temples. "We're close, Poppy. I can feel it. Kenneth's hiding something — but he's not the one pulling the strings. He's a pawn. A nervous, well-dressed pawn."

Poppy tapped the edge of her laptop, frustration plain on her face. "He's too careful to leave anything obvious out. If we're going to find anything real, we need to get into his office."

I blinked at her. "You want to break in?"

She didn't look up. "I want answers."

The answer came earlier than expected.

Dolly burst into the shop the next morning, cheeks red from the wind, a copy of the *Bloomwood Gazette* in hand like it was a golden ticket.

"He's out of town!" she announced, slapping the newspaper on the counter. "Kenneth's with Charlene at some fundraising thing in Greene County. His office should be totally empty tonight."

Poppy and I exchanged a glance—the same one we always shared when we were about to do something reckless... but morally justified.

It was the perfect opportunity.

The municipal building loomed in the fading light, its brick facade casting long shadows across the sidewalk. The parking lot was silent, the kind of quiet that made you nervous even if you weren't doing anything wrong.

I pulled my coat tighter. "Ready?"

Poppy nodded. "Let's do this."

Earlier that day, I'd sweet-talked the night janitor into leaving the side door unlocked with a blend of charm, mild panic, and a very convincing story about a missing invoice from a city flower contract.

We slipped in. The faint click of the door behind us echoed like a gunshot in the still hallway.

The building was dim, only a few flickering lights illuminating the stretch of beige linoleum and closed doors. We reached Kenneth's office, and I dropped to my knees, pulling a worn leather case from my coat pocket.

Poppy raised an eyebrow. "Seriously — when did you learn how to pick locks?"

"Don't ask questions you don't want the answers to," I muttered.

With a soft *click*, the lock gave way. We slid inside.

The office was exactly what I expected: pristine. Not a paperclip out of place. A half-full coffee mug sat beside an open notepad filled with Kenneth's tidy looping handwriting.

Poppy rifled through a drawer. "Nothing but calendars, budgets, and one overly confident stapler."

Then I saw it—a locked drawer at the bottom right corner of the desk.

"This one," I whispered, already setting to work again.

This lock was tougher, but the adrenaline was working in my favor. After a few tense seconds, *snick*—it opened.

Inside was a worn leather ledger.

I flipped it open and felt the breath leave my lungs.

Names. Dates. Payments.

Charles Dixon. Charlene Whitfield. Kenneth Marshall.

Poppy leaned over my shoulder. "It's a payoff list," she whispered. "Dixon was paying them."

"And Kenneth's name is in here more and more over the last few months." I flipped further. "The amounts keep going up."

Poppy pointed. "Dixon had something on him. He was trapped.

And Charlene? She was in deeper than anyone thought."

I scanned the pages. "But why was Dixon giving them money? What leverage did he have?"

"Maybe it started as mutual benefit," Poppy said, frowning. "Then things shifted. He wanted to expose her."

I turned to the final entry. The date? **Two days before the gala.**

"He was going to blow it all up," I said quietly. "This ledger — it's why he died."

A creak in the hallway froze us both.

Footsteps. Steady. Close.

I slammed the ledger shut and shoved it into my bag. We ducked against the wall, barely breathing.

A shadow passed across the frosted glass. Then paused.

My pulse thundered in my ears.

A few tense seconds later, the figure walked on.

Only then did we move. Bolting down the hallway, out the side door, and into the cold night air like it might burn away our fear.

Back at *Blossom & Thorne*, the shop was dark except for the soft glow of our desk lamp in the back. The familiar floral scents felt strange now — comforting and unnerving at once.

We laid the ledger open across the worktable, the inky names staring back like secrets finally unearthed.

Poppy rubbed her temples. "Kenneth was being paid off. Dixon had dirt on him. And now Charlene's trying to keep it all buried."

"And Dixon's dead," I said. "Which means someone cleaned up the loose end."

Before she could respond, the soft chime of the shop's front door echoed faintly from the next room.

Poppy and I looked at each other.

We weren't expecting anyone.

I stood slowly. "Did you lock the front door?"

She nodded. "You?"

I grabbed a nearby pair of floral shears — silly, but something solid — and we crept toward the front of the shop.

When we reached the showroom, no one was there.

Just the soft *click* of the front door swinging shut.

The street outside was empty.

Then I saw it.

A small slip of paper resting on the counter, just beneath the cash register.

I picked it up with shaking fingers.

The handwriting was slanted and jagged, hurried.

"Stay out of the Dixon business. Or you'll be next."

Poppy inhaled sharply behind me.

The note trembled in my hand. My throat went dry.

We looked out into the street again — still empty.

But someone had been here.

And now they knew we were getting too close.

Chapter 9

Cracks in the Mask

The dim kitchen light flickered above us, casting uneven shadows across the walls of our upstairs apartment. Poppy and I hunched over the battered leather ledger like it was a cursed object. The sharp scent of eucalyptus from the vase near the sink mingled with the stale coffee hanging in the air. Every so often, a car hummed past on the quiet street below, but inside, everything felt still. Heavy.

I tapped the ledger with my pen, frustration building. "It all comes back to Kenneth," I said. "He was juggling both Dixon and Charlene. But the wolfsbane — that's what doesn't add up. Why use something so traceable to us?"

Poppy stared at her mug. "Maybe he didn't plan to kill Dixon at all," she murmured. "What if he planted the wolfsbane to frame Charlene? A leverage play. Something he could hold over her if Dixon went public."

My eyes widened. "But something went wrong. Dixon must've figured it out. Confronted him."

Poppy nodded slowly. "Kenneth panicked. Maybe he never meant for it to go that far… but it spiraled."

I flipped through the ledger again. Each inked entry felt heavier than the last. "But if Kenneth acted alone, why would Charlene let him take the fall?"

Poppy's gaze sharpened. "She didn't let him. She told him to."

I looked up. "You think she planned it?"

"She benefits the most from Dixon's death. And Kenneth? He'd do anything for her."

A chill crawled down my spine.

We traced the timeline, cross-referencing entries in the ledger. One note near the bottom stopped us cold:

"Confirm delivery — last chance."

"That's her," I whispered. "She pushed him to act before Dixon could go public."

Poppy sat back. "Kenneth was supposed to clean it up. But when Dixon didn't die quietly… the whole thing blew up."

I ran a finger down the list of names and numbers. "We need Kenneth to talk," I said. "He's the weak link."

The next morning, Dolly swept into the shop like a woman on a mission.

"Kenneth has a standing coffee break at Maggie's Café," she said, sliding her bag off her shoulder. "Same time, same table, every week. Today's your chance."

"How do you know all of this stuff?" Poppy asked Dolly.

"I was just talking to some of the ladies at the hair salon yesterday and Fannie Johnson, said her cousin always sees Kenneth at Maggie's Cafe same time everyday."

I thought that made sense, small town, everyone knows everything about everybody.

Poppy and I looked at each other, both thinking the same thing.

Showtime.

The café was warm and golden, filled with the smell of buttered croissants and spiced coffee. But we weren't there for pastries.

We claimed a corner table with a perfect view of the door, hearts racing beneath our calm exteriors.

Kenneth walked in minutes later, looking more rumpled than usual. His shoulders were stiff, his eyes shadowed.

I rose from my seat and approached his table. "Good morning, Mr. Marshall."

His eyes flicked toward the exit. Before he could move, Poppy slid into the seat across from him and gently placed the ledger on the table.

Kenneth froze.

His hand trembled as he reached for his coffee. "What is this?"

"Proof," Poppy said evenly. "Of everything. Payments from Dixon. Your ties to Charlene. And the mess that followed."

"You don't know what you're talking about," he said, voice tight.

"We know more than you think," I said. "You planted the wolfsbane to frame Charlene. But Dixon figured it out — and you panicked."

The polished mask cracked.

"I didn't kill him," Kenneth whispered, his fingers gripping the edge of the table. "I couldn't go through with it."

Poppy leaned in. "Then what was the plan? Were you going to blackmail Charlene? Or was this her idea from the beginning?"

He closed his eyes, his voice fraying. "Charlene wanted Dixon silenced. She told me to scare him… plant something. Something toxic, to shake him. It was never supposed to go that far."

I exchanged a glance with Poppy.

Kenneth looked up, haunted. "I couldn't do it. I left the gala early. But when I heard he was dead—"

His voice caught.

"I don't know who she got to finish the job," he said. "But it wasn't me."

Poppy's eyes narrowed. "You seriously expect us to believe she handed off a murder plot to someone else and didn't tell you?"

He gave a hollow laugh. "You don't know Charlene. If you're not useful anymore, you're replaceable. And dangerous."

I sat back, processing. "So who else is working with her?"

Kenneth shook his head. "I don't know. But I guarantee she has someone."

We rose from the table slowly, minds reeling.

"She's letting you take the fall," Poppy said softly.

Kenneth didn't respond. His head dropped into his hands. "If you go after her... she'll destroy you."

Poppy and I turned toward the door.

"We're not afraid of Charlene Whitfield," she said over her shoulder.

Outside, the air was crisp and bright. The moment we stepped into the street, I felt the weight of our next move pressing in like a storm front.

"She's not working alone," I said.

Poppy nodded. "Then we find out who is."

Chapter 10

Garden Hints and Handwritten Clues

The Bloomwood Community Church was wrapped in a quiet stillness that felt too heavy for a breezy fall afternoon. Poppy and I stood on the stone path that curved around to the back garden, where Reverend

Michael Robinson liked to tend his flowers after morning service.

He looked up as we approached, wiping his hands on a worn cloth and flashing that calm, disarming smile of his. "Ladies. What brings the Thorne sisters to my humble little plot of peace?"

"Just needed a breath of something besides mystery," Poppy said, scanning the flower beds. "Though I've gotta say... you have an interesting choice of flora."

My gaze followed hers — straight to a cluster of striking purple flowers.

Wolfsbane.

Poppy raised an eyebrow. "You do know that's poisonous, right?"

Reverend Robinson chuckled softly, returning to his pruning. "Everything has the potential to be dangerous if used the wrong way. But admire it from a distance? It's just another beautiful bloom. Like people, really."

His words hung in the air, delicate and unsettling all at once.

I forced a smile. "Still, not exactly a common flower to grow in your average church garden."

He shrugged. "I appreciate rare things."

We traded glances—Poppy's look said exactly what I was thinking: cryptic much?

As if sensing the shift in energy, Michael stood up straighter. "Dixon was a complicated man. But he loved this town. You know he left a sizable donation to the church in his will?"

Poppy blinked. "Really?"

He nodded, adjusting his gloves. "We're grateful, of course. His generosity will help us expand the youth programs."

That was the moment something clicked—because a donation like that could easily be motive. Or hush money. Or both.

"Thanks for your time, Reverend," I said, my voice a bit tighter than before.

We walked away slowly, our minds racing.

"So… poison in the flower beds, vague philosophy about danger, and a surprise inheritance?" Poppy muttered as we turned the corner. "I'm not saying he did it, but I'm also not saying he's not at the top of my suspect list now."

"Agreed," I said. "Let's clear our heads over lunch."

Maggie's Café smelled like cinnamon and melted butter, the kind of aroma that usually made everything feel safe.

Not today.

Scott was already waiting for us at a window table. The minute he saw us, his expression shifted — half concern, half husband-mode.

He pulled out a chair for me. "Okay. What's going on now?"

Poppy wordlessly slid the crumpled note across the table.

Scott unfolded it, his brow furrowing with each word. "You didn't tell me about this," he said, his voice dropping to a whisper. "Iris—this is serious. You have a son. Poppy, we have a daughter. Do you two remember your family? This isn't just about clearing your name anymore."

"We're being careful," I said, though the knot in my stomach said otherwise.

Scott wasn't buying it. "You're not detectives. And whoever left this note is willing to threaten you. That means they're already desperate. And that means danger."

"We know," Poppy said gently.

"It's noble what you're doing," he continued, "but it's time to loop in Detective Tyler. Let the professionals do their job."

I exhaled. "You're right."

"We promise," Poppy added.

Scott relaxed just a fraction and stood to grab the check. As he walked to the counter, Maggie appeared, her usual no-nonsense energy wrapped in an apron and sarcasm.

"Well now. Don't you three look like a secret task force," she said with a smirk, dropping the bill in front of me.

As I reached for it, something made me pause.

The handwriting.

My heart skipped.

"Poppy," I said under my breath. "Look at this."

She leaned over, eyes narrowing. "That looks exactly like the note."

Quick as ever, she pulled out her phone and snapped a photo.

Maggie's smile dimmed, just for a second. "Problem?"

"Nope," I said sweetly. "Just admiring your penmanship."

She arched a brow, but didn't press.

Scott gave us both a kiss on the cheek, his eyes still laced with worry. "Please… just be careful."

"We will," we said in unison.

But the second he left the café, we exchanged that look again—the one we always gave each other right before we did something impulsive.

"We're coming back here tonight," Poppy whispered.

The café was quieter when we returned, the golden lights casting long shadows across the tables.

Maggie was behind the counter, humming to herself and sweeping with practiced ease.

"Oh, you two again?" she said, flashing a grin. "Did the muffins call your names or are you just stalking me now?"

"Blueberry," Poppy said, pointing to the display.

While she made our "order," my eyes wandered—and then landed on a small flask tucked just behind the napkin holder.

Wolfsbane. Clear as day, in fine print.

Maggie noticed. "Headache remedy. Just a few drops, totally diluted. Old homeopathic trick. You wouldn't believe how well it works."

Poppy didn't blink. "Odd choice for a café."

Maggie's tone sharpened. "Are you accusing me of something?"

"We found a note," I said. "And the handwriting matches the one you gave us at lunch."

Her lips tightened. "I didn't poison anyone, if that's what you're suggesting."

"Then why leave a threatening note?" Poppy asked.

Maggie sighed and leaned in, voice dropping. "Because I heard what people were saying. You two snooping around, asking questions like this was a game. Dixon was private. I didn't want his name dragged through town gossip."

"So you were protecting him?" I asked.

"Protecting myself," she said flatly. "He was my investor. Without him, this café would've folded. But lately, he'd been pressuring me to expand. Go franchise. I said no, and he threatened to pull out. We fought. Loudly. I know how it looked."

Poppy's gaze moved to the flask again. "And the wolfsbane?"

"Diluted," Maggie said firmly. "It wouldn't kill a fly."

We left the café without saying much else. The cool night air pressed in around us like a second skin.

"She has motive," Poppy said softly. "Dixon pulling out would ruin her. She had a reason."

"And she definitely wasn't honest with us before," I added.

Poppy zipped her coat. "That tea, the note, the arguments… she's moved to the top of my list."

I nodded. "Ours just got shorter."

Chapter 11

A Confession Waiting to Happen

The low hum of the shop's heater barely cut through the tension filling Blossom & Thorne. The usual comforting scent of lilies and eucalyptus felt heavier now, clinging to the corners of the room like nerves waiting to snap.

Fresh bouquets lined the windows. Ribbons were curled and baskets fluffed. It all looked perfect — on the surface.

But today, our little flower shop was more than a sanctuary.

It was a trap.

Poppy adjusted the bouquet on the counter, fingers twitching just slightly. I checked the hidden recording device nestled behind a cluster of forget-me-nots. Its red light blinked once, then settled. Live.

"Do you think they'll all come?" she whispered.

"They'll come," I said, my voice low but sure. "They each think they're about to be exposed."

And they were right.

It had taken days of digging, questioning, dodging threats, and following instincts we didn't know we had. And strangely enough, it was Mrs. Bosley, of all people, who cracked the case open—while casually chatting with Dolly about her Snowville church retreat.

"Oh, Reverend Robinson was wonderful," Mrs. Bosley had said, her voice lilting. "He preached twice that weekend. Can you believe that? Two sermons in one trip! We were up in Snowville from Friday morning till late Sunday. A peaceful little getaway."

Dolly, always curious, asked when the retreat had taken place.

Mrs. Bosley smiled. "The weekend of the gala, dear. We left right before that fancy event in town."

Poppy and I had exchanged a look. Reverend Robinson was out of town the night of the murder. Which meant he was officially off the suspect list.

But that still left Kenneth, Charlene, and Maggie — all tangled in Dixon's messy web of money, secrets, and betrayal.

So we set a plan in motion.

A fake note.

A whispered threat.

And a promise that someone in the room knew the whole story.

The bell above the shop door jingled.

Kenneth Marshall entered first, his overcoat flapping with the force of his nerves. His hair was slicked back

too neatly, his eyes scanning the shop
like it might bite him.

Behind him came Charlene
Whitfield, as polished as ever. She
wore her power like perfume—bold
and unmistakable—but something
about her posture gave her away. She
was unsure.

Last came Maggie Bishop, wiping
her hands on a café apron as if she'd
come straight from rolling pastry
dough.

They didn't speak at first.

Poppy and I stood behind the
counter like florists ready to take an

order, not amateur sleuths about to spring a trap.

"I assume you didn't call us here for daisies," Charlene said coolly.

Kenneth was already sweating.

And Maggie? She said nothing. Just stared at the wrapped bouquet on the counter — the one with a single purple wolfsbane bloom tucked among the eucalyptus.

"You all had reasons to want Charles Dixon gone," I said calmly. "But only one of you actually followed through."

Poppy laid the folder on the counter. "Ledger entries. The threatening note. The flask. The arguments. The handwriting. The motive."

Kenneth opened his mouth, but for once, no words came out.

Charlene arched a brow. "Is this some sort of dramatic stunt?"

Before I could answer, the bell jingled again—and Detective Jennifer Tyler walked in with two officers behind her.

"This isn't a stunt," she said, her voice sharp and clear. "It's a confession waiting to happen."

The room stiffened.

Kenneth crumbled first.

"I didn't do it," he blurted. "Yes, I covered for Charlene. Yes, I panicked. But I couldn't go through with it. I never touched the wolfsbane — I didn't even know where it came from!"

Charlene narrowed her eyes at him. "Covered for me? You thought I wanted him dead?"

"You said —" Kenneth stammered. "You told me to take him out. I thought you meant it!"

Charlene scoffed. "It was a joke, Kenneth. A bad one. But a joke. I didn't want you to kill Charles."

And then all eyes turned to Maggie.

She stood frozen, lips pressed into a line. Her eyes glistened, but her jaw stayed firm.

When she finally spoke, her voice was low. "He broke my heart."

No one moved.

Maggie looked at Detective Tyler. "It wasn't supposed to go that far. I just wanted him scared. Wanted him to stop threatening to pull out of the café.

THORNE SISTERS COZY MYSTERY: PETALS, POISON, AND PERIL

He was more than just an investor. We… had a history."

Poppy and I both stilled.

"A relationship?" I asked gently.

Maggie nodded. "An old one. Private. But recently… he ended it. Said he'd found someone else. Wanted to cut ties completely. Personally. Financially. Privately." She exhaled shakily. "I couldn't let him humiliate me. Not after everything."

Tyler stepped forward. "You laced his drink at the gala?"

"I brought him tea," Maggie whispered. "He always said it helped his stomach when he drank too much wine. I only used a little wolfsbane. I guess it was too much. I didn't think—"

She stopped herself.

There was nothing else to say.

Tyler gave a quiet nod to her officers.

As the cuffs clicked shut around Maggie's wrists, she didn't resist.

Charlene turned to Poppy and me, her face unusually sober. "I meant what I said earlier. I didn't like Dixon. But I never wanted him dead." She turned to Kenneth. "And you—never act on a joke again."

Kenneth looked like he might throw up.

The officers led Maggie out, and with them went the weight of weeks of suspicion, anxiety, and unanswered questions.

Tyler stayed behind for a moment longer, her gaze resting on the shop's familiar surroundings.

"You both did good work," she said. "Risky. But good."

I gave a tired smile. "We'd rather go back to arranging peonies."

Poppy groaned softly. "After a nap. Maybe two."

Tyler smiled, then tipped her head. "Take the day. You've earned it."

And just like that, the shop fell quiet again.

For the first time in what felt like forever… it felt like ours.

Poppy sank into the chair behind the register, rubbing her temples. "So… Maggie and Dixon… in a relationship. Well, I didn't see that coming."

I looked around at the soft glow of the shop lights, the perfect rows of blooms, the vase of newly delivered tulips waiting to be arranged.

"I didn't either," I said. "But I'm glad it's over."

And this time… it really was.

Chapter 12

Petals of Justice

Morning sunlight streamed through the large windows of *Blossom & Thorne*, casting a golden glow across the shop. The light played off the delicate petals of the bouquets arranged in neat rows, illuminating shades of blush pink, buttery yellow, and deep violet. The familiar fragrance of roses, freesia, and lavender mingled with the rich scent of coffee from the mugs perched on the worktable.

I stood at the counter, carefully adjusting a cluster of daisies in a vibrant centerpiece for the town library's anniversary celebration. Each petal was perfectly placed, a stark contrast to the chaos of the past few weeks.

Across from me, Poppy perched on a stool, wrapping the stems of a bouquet in soft brown parchment paper.

"For the first time in forever," she mused, tucking a loose dahlia into place, "I don't feel like someone's watching our every move."

I chuckled, securing the last of the stems. "Don't be so sure. Half the town is probably peeking through these windows, trying to catch a glimpse of Bloomwood's accidental detectives."

She smirked. "You mean *heroes*."

The bell above the door jingled, and Dolly waltzed in, balancing a tray of steaming coffees. The rich aroma of espresso curled into the air, adding a warmth that blended with the scent of fresh blooms.

"Morning, *heroes*," she teased, setting the tray on the counter. "How does it feel to be Bloomwood's most talked-about duo?"

"Exhausting," Poppy said with a laugh, grabbing a cup. "But at least it's better than being accused of murder."

Dolly snorted. "Low bar, but fair point." She leaned against the counter, her expression turning curious. "Any updates on Maggie?"

I nodded, my smile fading slightly. "Detective Tyler stopped by yesterday. Maggie's being charged with manslaughter."

"Good riddance." Dolly shook her head, taking a sip of her coffee. "I still can't believe she thought she could pull it off."

Poppy carefully arranged a cluster of lilies in the centerpiece, her fingers brushing over the silky petals. "She almost did. If Kenneth hadn't cracked, he'd still be under suspicion." She glanced at me. "It's unsettling how close we came to losing everything."

I placed the final bloom — a striking orange gerbera daisy — into the arrangement and stepped back, admiring our work. The centerpiece radiated warmth and vibrancy, a stark contrast to the weight of the past weeks.

"It's over now," I said softly. "We can finally focus on what we love — flowers, not investigations."

Before Poppy could respond, Scott came downstairs into the flower shop with Violet in tow, her tiny hand gripping his as she skipped behind him. Phillip followed, looking only mildly interested in whatever had dragged him into the shop this early.

Scott surveyed the shop with exaggerated interest. "So, this is the headquarters of Bloomwood's top detectives. Quite the setup."

"Very professional," Phillip added, squinting at a neatly stacked pile of invoices like it held the secrets to the universe.

I smirked. "Yes, we've gone back to our true calling — flower arranging. No more mysteries, just petals and peace."

"Petals and peace," Scott repeated with a chuckle. "I like the sound of that."

Violet, bouncing on her heels, beamed up at me. "Can I be a detective too?"

Dolly leaned down, whispering conspiratorially. "I don't know, Violet. It's a dangerous business."

Violet gasped dramatically. "Like *super* dangerous?"

"Very," Poppy said, eyes twinkling. "Secret meetings, coded messages, scary villains."

Violet's eyes widened. "Ooooh. Can I have a code name?"

Phillip, leaning against the counter, smirked. "I vote for *Agent Sprinkles*."

Scott snorted into his coffee as Violet stamped her foot. "No way! That's not cool enough."

"How about *Shadow Rose*?" I suggested, winking.

Violet's face lit up with delight. "Yes! I'm *Shadow Rose*! And I will solve all the mysteries of Bloomwood!"

Dolly nudged Poppy. "Give it a week. She'll have a notebook full of suspects."

"I'd expect nothing less," Poppy said, laughing.

Scott gave me a knowing look. "All joking aside, I hope you two are done with the detective work for good."

I nodded. "Trust me, so do we."

"Good," he said. "Because next time, I'm charging for emotional damages."

"Oh, please," I said, rolling my eyes. "You loved every minute of it."

Scott lifted his coffee cup in mock agreement. "Sure. But next time, I expect a sidekick salary."

The playful conversation was interrupted by the bell jingling once more. Mrs. Carmichael, one of our most loyal customers, stepped inside, her smile as warm as the morning sun.

"Good morning, dears," she greeted, clutching her purse. "I just wanted to tell you how proud the whole town is of you. You've made Bloomwood proud."

A genuine warmth spread through me. "Thank you, Mrs. Carmichael. That means so much to us."

She patted my hand affectionately. "And I do hope you'll be at the town celebration next week. We want to properly honor you two."

Poppy and I exchanged a glance, amusement flickering between us. "We wouldn't miss it," she promised.

As Mrs. Carmichael left, Poppy turned to me, her voice thoughtful. "You know, for all the chaos, I think we've come out of this stronger. The shop's never been busier, and we've proven we can handle more than just flowers."

I chuckled, leaning against the counter. "True. But let's hope our future challenges involve roses and peonies—not poison, police and peril."

Dolly clinked her coffee cup against mine. "Amen to that."

For the first time in weeks, I felt a deep sense of peace settle over me. The weight that had hung over us seemed to lift with each passing moment.

I glanced around the shop, taking in the sight of fresh blooms, warm sunlight, and the people I cared about most.

"Back to normal," I murmured.

"Almost," Poppy said with a smirk. "But we *did* learn one thing."

I raised an eyebrow. "What's that?"

Her eyes sparkled. "Always keep an eye out for the unexpected. You never know what secrets might bloom."

I laughed, my shoulders finally relaxing. "True. But for now, let's enjoy the peace while it lasts."

As another customer entered, we turned back to work, hands moving deftly through petals and stems, shaping beauty from chaos.

Life in Bloomwood was returning to normal, but I knew one thing for sure—Poppy and I weren't the same as before. We had uncovered the truth, faced danger head-on, and come out the other side stronger.

Each flower we arranged felt like a quiet victory, a symbol of resilience. Whatever challenges lay ahead, I knew one thing:

We were ready.

ABOUT THE AUTHOR

D.G. Thomas began her writing journey with *The Magic Chest: Sands of Time*, inspired by the bedtime stories she shared with her children. Since then, she has written and published three more books in *The Magic Chest* series — *Dancing 'Til Dusk, Halloween Hideout*, and *Seaside Treasure* — as well as the picture books *Norris and Twig* and *The Flower Power Unicorns*.

Expanding beyond children's literature, Thomas now writes for audiences of all ages, including mystery lovers. She is the author of the *Thorne Sisters Cozy Mystery Series*, bringing her signature storytelling style to intriguing small-town whodunits.

A graduate of the University of Louisville and a member of the Society of Children's Book Writers and Illustrators, Thomas resides in Kentucky — where the grass isn't really blue — with her daughter, son, and their ever-curious cat.

Follow her on Instagram, Facebook, and X, and learn more at authordgthomas.com.

Thorne Sisters Cozy Mystery Series

Petals, Poison and Peril

Bouquets, Betrayal, and Burial

Dahlia's, Deceit, and Doom

Orchids, Obsession, and Omens

Roses, Revenge, and Ruin

Made in United States
Cleveland, OH
20 April 2025

16245574R00107